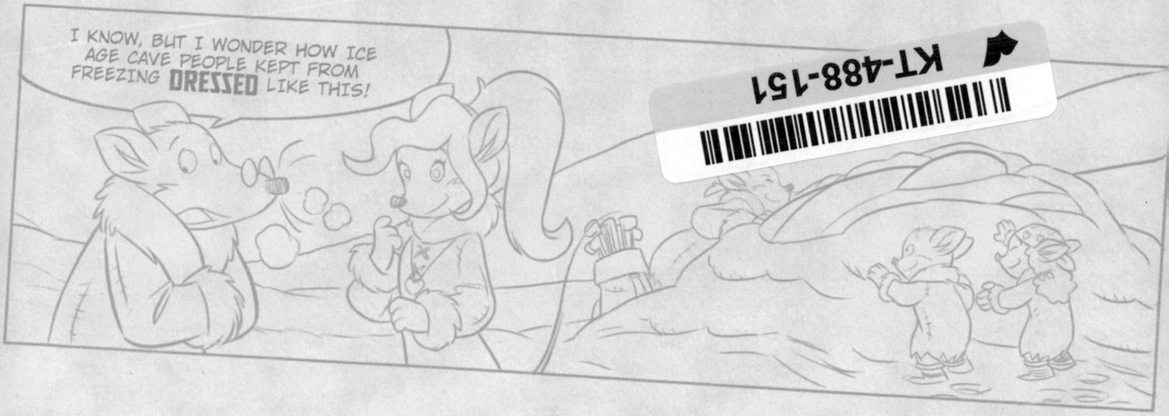
I KNOW, BUT I WONDER HOW ICE AGE CAVE PEOPLE KEPT FROM FREEZING DRESSED LIKE THIS!

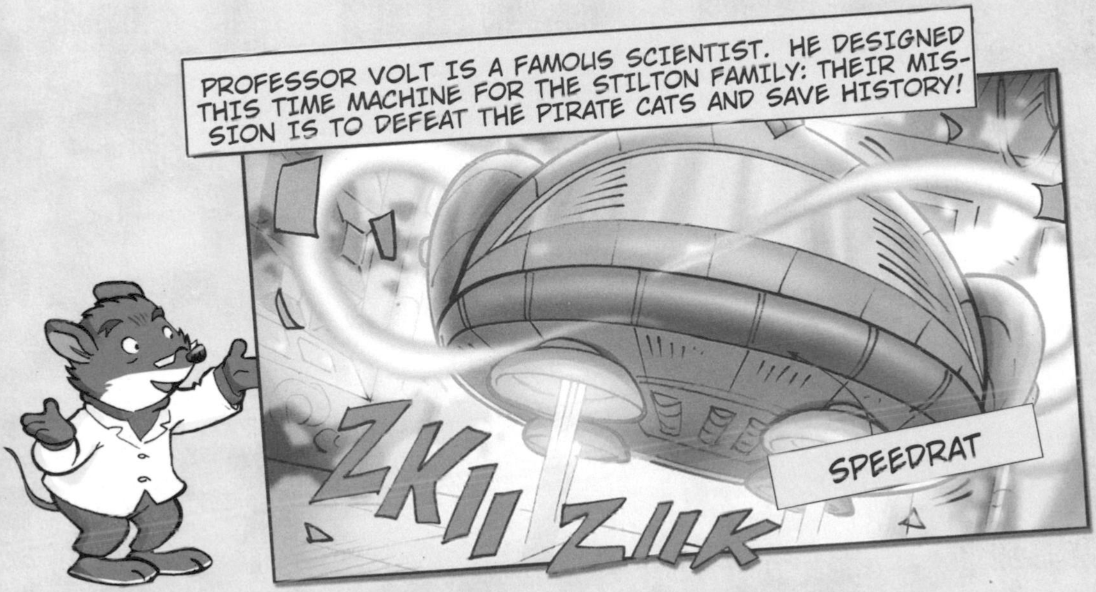
PROFESSOR VOLT IS A FAMOUS SCIENTIST. HE DESIGNED THIS TIME MACHINE FOR THE STILTON FAMILY: THEIR MISSION IS TO DEFEAT THE PIRATE CATS AND SAVE HISTORY!
SPEEDRAT
ZKII ZIIK

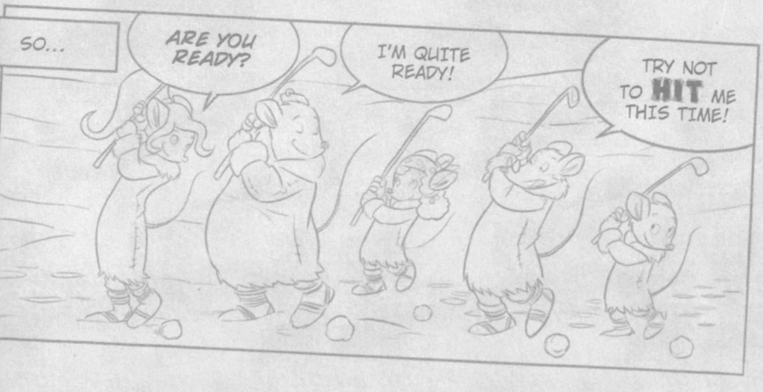
SO...
ARE YOU READY?
I'M QUITE READY!
TRY NOT TO HIT ME THIS TIME!

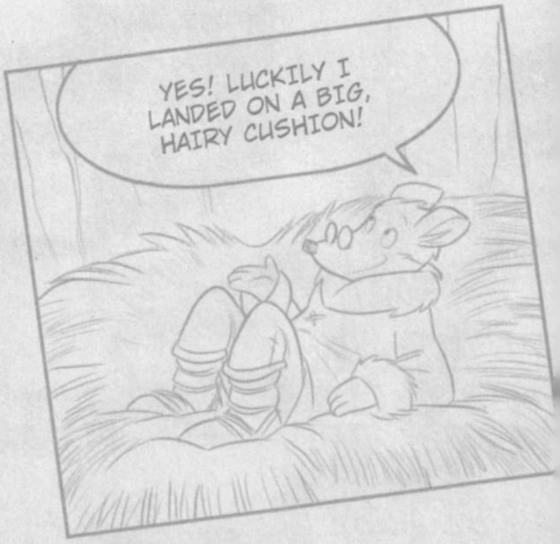
YES! LUCKILY I LANDED ON A BIG, HAIRY CUSHION!

Geronimo Stilton

THE GREAT ICE AGE

PAPERCUT**Z**™

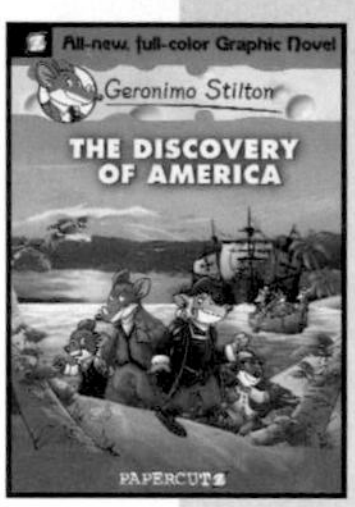
All-new, full-color Graphic Novel
Geronimo Stilton
THE DISCOVERY OF AMERICA
PAPERCUTZ

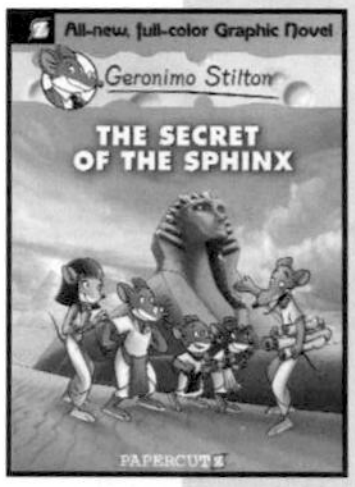
All-new, full-color Graphic Novel
Geronimo Stilton
THE SECRET OF THE SPHINX
PAPERCUTZ

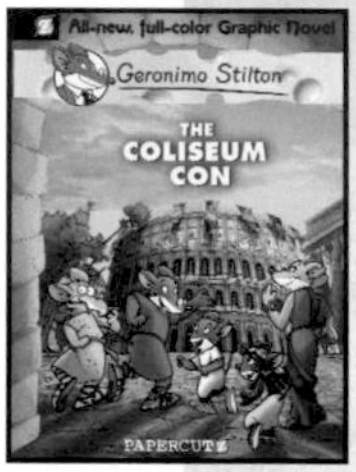
All-new, full-color Graphic Novel
Geronimo Stilton
THE COLISEUM CON
PAPERCUTZ

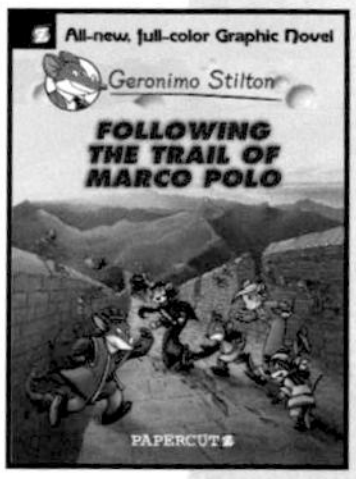
All-new, full-color Graphic Novel
Geronimo Stilton
FOLLOWING THE TRAIL OF MARCO POLO
PAPERCUTZ

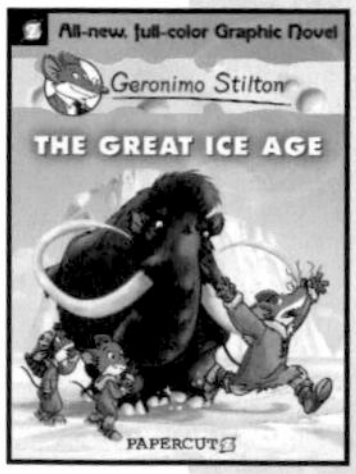
All-new, full-color Graphic Novel
Geronimo Stilton
THE GREAT ICE AGE
PAPERCUTZ

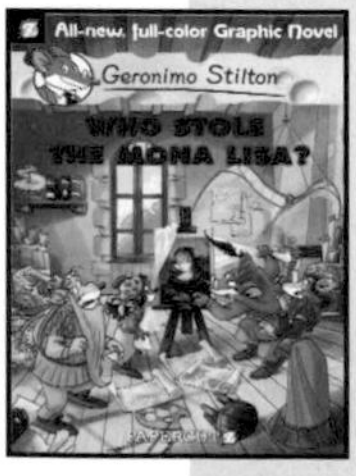
All-new, full-color Graphic Novel
Geronimo Stilton
WHO STOLE THE MONA LISA?

Geronimo Stilton

GRAPHIC NOVELS AVAILABLE FROM PAPERCUTZ™

Graphic Novel #1
"The Discovery of America"

Graphic Novel #2
"The Secret of the Sphinx"

Graphic Novel #3
"The Coliseum Con"

Graphic Novel #4
"Following the Trail of Marco Polo"

Graphic Novel #5
"The Great Ice Age"

Coming Soon:
Graphic Novel #6
"Who Stole The Mona Lisa?"

Geronimo Stilton graphic novels are available in hardcover for $9.99 each. Please add $4.00 for postage and handling for the first book, add $1.00 for each additional book. Please make check payable to NBM Publishing.
Send to:
Papercutz, 40 Exchange Place,
Suite 1308,
New York, NY 10005
1-800-886-1223

www.papercutz.com

Geronimo Stilton

THE GREAT ICE AGE

By Geronimo Stilton

New York

THE GREAT ICE AGE
© EDIZIONI PIEMME 2008 S.p.A.
Via Tiziano 32, 20145
Milan, Italy
Geronimo Stilton names, characters and related indicia are copyright,
trademark and exclusive license of Atlantyca S.p.A.
All rights reserved.
The moral right of the author has been asserted.

Text by Geronimo Stilton
Editorial coordination by Patrizia Puricelli
Original editing by Daniela Finistauri
Script by Demetrio Bargellini
Based on an original idea by Elisabetta Dami
Artistic coordination by Roberta Bianchi
Artistic assistance by Tommaso Valsecchi
Graphic Project by Michela Battaglin
Graphics by Marta Lorini
Cover art and color by Flavio Ferron
Interior illustrations by Wasabi! Studio and color by Davide Turotti

© 2010 – for this work in English language by Papercutz.

Original title: Geronimo Stilton La Grande Era Glaciale

Translation by: Nanette McGuinness

www.geronimostilton.com

Stilton is the name of a famous English cheese. It is a registered trademark of the
Stilton Cheese Makers' Association. For more information go to:
www.stiltoncheese.com

Lettering and Production by Ortho
Michael Petranek – Editorial Assistant
Jim Salicrup
Editor-in-Chief

ISBN: 978-1-59707-202-1

Printed in China.
March 2010 by WKT Co. LTD.
3/F Phase 1 Leader Industrial Centre
188 Texaco Road, Tsuen Wan, N.T.
Hong Kong

Distributed by Macmillan.
10 9 8 7 6 5 4 3 2 1

IT WAS A PEACEFUL **SUNNY** MORNING AND I FOUND MYSELF AT THE NEW MOUSE CITY GOLF COURSE...

...WITH MY NEPHEW BENJAMIN, MY FRIEND PATTY SPRING, AND MY NIECE PANDORA.

EXCUSE ME, I HAVEN'T INTRODUCED MYSELF YET: MY NAME IS STILTON, *Geronimo Stilton!* AND I EDIT THE RODENT'S GAZETTE, THE MOST FAMOUS PAPER ON MOUSE ISLAND!

DON'T BOTHER TAKING IT, GERONIMO. YOU CAN SEE THE NEXT SHOT WILL BE BETTER!

YOU'RE SO NICE, PATTY!

YOU KNOW, I'VE WANTED TO SPEND A BIT OF TIME WITH YOU FOR SO LONG...

...WELL, HERE...WHAT I WANT TO SAY IS THAT WHEN WE'RE TOGETHER, I...

WAKE UP, GRANDSON!!!!

SQUEEEAK!

GRANDPA TANK?!? WHAT ARE YOU DOING HERE?

I'M PLAYING WITH MY FRIEND, LONGSHOT PUTTER, DIRECTOR OF THE NEW MOUSE CITY SUBWAY!

GOOD MORNING!

HELLO, GERONIMO!

BUT YOU, HOWEVER, WHY AREN'T YOU AT WORK?

WELL, HERE'S...

WHEN I RAN THE PAPER, I WOULD NEVER HAVE DREAMED OF TAKING A DAY OFF, NEVER!

6

BUT GRANDPA, TODAY'S SUNDAY, SO I THOUGHT I'D...

I KNOW PERFECTLY WELL WHAT DAY IT IS, JUST LIKE I KNOW PERFECTLY WELL THAT YOU'RE A LAZYPAWS!

ENJOY YOUR GAME, BUT I WANT AN ARTICLE ON GOLF TOMORROW!

>SIGH!< I'VE GOT A FEELING I'M DONE RELAXING FOR TODAY!

WHEN GRANDPA TANK HAD GONE AWAY...

WONDERFUL SHOT, UNCLE!

THE BALL SOARED AWAY AS FAR AS THE EYE CAN SEE!

A LITTLE TOO FAR! I'M NOT SURE I KNOW WHICH DIRECTION IT WENT!

SQUEEEAK!

OOPS! SORRY, COUSIN, I GAUGED THE TRAJECTORY OF MY SHOT BADLY!

TRAP!?!

I DIDN'T KNOW YOU LIKED TO PLAY GOLF!

I DON'T JUST LIKE IT: I'M A CHAMPION!

THE SECRET TO GOLF IS TO PLACE THE BALL ON THE GROUND WELL...

...AND THEN HIT IT WITH ALL THE POWER YOU'VE GOT!

SWWISSSSHH

SPLAFF

GERONIMO, ARE YOU OKAY?

UM...YES...

SEE, COUSIN? I'M A REAL CHAMPION!

8

WELL, YES...ALL IN ALL...MAYBE THE SHOT WASN'T VERY ACCURATE...

...BUT THE IMPORTANT THING IS NOT TO GET DISCOURAGED AND TO TRY AGAIN RIGHT AWAY!

>GULP!<

QUICK, EVERYONE TAKE COVER!

!?

WATCH AND LEARN, COUSIN!

SLAM

>PUFF, PANT...PUFF, PANT!<

HELP!!!

SOCK

SQUEAK!

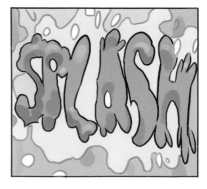

SPLASH

9

POOR ME, I REALLY WOULD'VE BEEN BETTER OFF GOING TO THE OFFICE TODAY!

RIBBIT, RIBBIT, RIBBIT!

UM...COULD YOU GET OFF MY HEAD?

BUT OF COURSE, GERONIMO!

MOLDY MOZZARELLA! A TALKING FROG?!

THIS FROG IS ACTUALLY A LITTLE ROBOT!

B-B-BUT...THAT VOICE... PROFESSOR VOLT, IS THAT YOU?

INDEED, IT IS! THIS FROG IS MY LATEST INVENTION. PRETTY NICE, DON'T YOU THINK? I MANAGED TO TRACK YOU DOWN WITH IT.

I NEED TO SEE YOU AND YOUR FRIENDS...HISTORY IS IN DANGER!

>GULP!< IF THAT'S THE CASE, PROFESSOR, WE'LL BE **RIGHT THERE!**

A HALF HOUR LATER, WE WERE IN PATTY'S SUV, FOLLOWING THE FROG ROBOT'S DIRECTIONS...

AT THE NEXT LIGHT, TURN RIGHT!

...WHICH QUICKLY TOOK US TO AMPY VOLT'S SECRET LAB!

HELLO, PROFESSOR! TELL US EVERYTHING!

ARE THE **PIRATE CATS** BEHIND THIS?

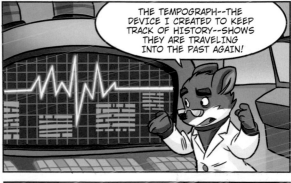

THE TEMPOGRAPH--THE DEVICE I CREATED TO KEEP TRACK OF HISTORY--SHOWS THEY ARE TRAVELING INTO THE PAST AGAIN!

UNFORTUNATELY, YES, GERONIMO. YOU GUESSED RIGHT!

AND WHERE ARE THEY HEADED THIS TIME? HAVE YOU FIGURED IT OUT YET, PROFESSOR?

THAT'S THE STRANGE THING: THEIR DESTINATION IS THE NEANDER VALLEY IN GERMANY, AROUND 40,000 YEARS AGO!

40,000 YEARS AGO? BUT THAT WAS DURING THE **PLEISTOCENE!**

PLEISTOCENE

IN THIS GEOLOGICAL ERA (1,800,000–11,000 YEARS AGO) THE EARTH LOOKED A LOT DIFFERENT FROM TODAY. AS A MATTER OF FACT, THE PLEISTOCENE WAS CHARACTERIZED BY THE CLIMATE CONSTANTLY GETTING COLDER, WHICH CAUSED THE NORTH POLE ICE SHEET AND GLACIERS FROM THE MOUNTAINS TO INVADE MOST OF NORTH AMERICA AND EUROPE. THIS PHENOMENON IS KNOWN AS GLACIATION AND WAS THE START OF THE ICE AGE. THE AREAS SHELTERED FROM ICE, LIKE THE NEANDER VALLEY (NEANDERTHAL) IN NORTHERN GERMANY, WERE FILLED WITH GRASSLANDS AND FORESTS IN WHICH MANY SPECIES OF WILD ANIMALS (DEER, BEAR, WOLVES, MARMOTS, AND MAMMOTHS) AND THE ANCESTORS OF MODERN HUMANS LIVED.

IF I'M NOT WRONG, THERE WEREN'T ANY CITIES IN THIS ERA, ONLY FORESTS!

YES, THAT'S RIGHT! AND WIDE GRASSLANDS, TOO!

HMM...A PERFECT PLACE TO PLAY GOLF! HOW NICE!

HMPH, TRAP...HOW CAN YOU THINK OF PLAYING RIGHT NOW?

BETTER YET, DO YOU HAVE ANY IDEA WHAT THE PIRATE CATS' GOAL COULD BE?

NO, NO IDEA AT ALL!

THE AREA BORDERED BY THE **ICE** SHEET WAS PRACTICALLY UNINHABITED, EXCEPT FOR...EARLY NEANDERTHALS!

EARLY NEANDERTHALS

LIVED BETWEEN 100,000 AND 30,000 YEARS AGO. THEIR NAME COMES FROM THE FACT THAT IN 1856, SOME OF THEIR REMAINS WERE FOUND IN A CAVE IN THE NEANDER VALLEY. COMPARED TO MODERN HUMANS (HOMO SAPIENS), NEANDERTHALS WERE SHORTER AND HAD SHORTER ARMS AND LEGS. THEIR TYPICAL FACIAL FEATURES WERE A LOW, FLAT SKULL, PRONOUNCED CHEEKBONES, AND A RECEDING CHIN.

WHATEVER THOSE CRUMMY CATS MAY HAVE IN MIND, WE'VE GOT TO LEAVE RIGHT AWAY!

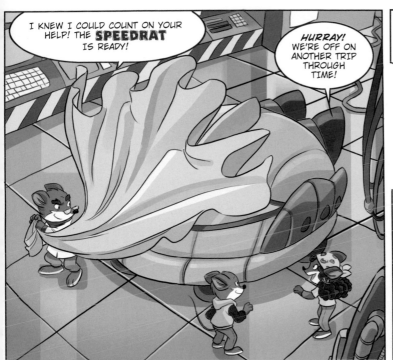

I KNEW I COULD COUNT ON YOUR HELP! THE **SPEEDRAT** IS READY!

HURRAY! WE'RE OFF ON ANOTHER TRIP THROUGH TIME!

I'M GIVING YOU MY SPECIAL EARPHONES THAT LET YOU SPEAK AND UNDERSTAND THE LANGUAGE OF THE TIME!

I'LL PUT MY GOLF BAG NEXT TO THE CLOTHES WE'LL WEAR WHEN WE GET THERE!

PLEASE KEEP THE PIRATE CATS FROM CHANGING HISTORY TO BENEFIT THEMSELVES!

DON'T WORRY, PROFESSOR, WE'LL STOP THEM!

ZZZZZZZZLKKK

TAKE-OFFFF!!!

MEANWHILE, THE PIRATE CATS HAD ARRIVED IN THE NEANDER VALLEY IN THE YEAR 37993 BC.

THIS TIME, YOU'VE REALLY MESSED UP, BONZO!

B-BUT TERSILLA, LET ME EXPLAIN! I...UM...

THERE'S NOTHING TO EXPLAIN! OUR DESTINATION WAS PARIS, IN FRANCE, IN THE YEAR 1889...AND LOOK WHERE YOU BROUGHT US!

BUT I DIDN'T MEAN TO...I WAS TAKING SOME SOUVENIR PHOTOS AND...I HIT THE WRONG BUTTON!

BONZO, YOU ARE A REAL IDIOT!

I DON'T CARE ABOUT SOME PHOTO! WE WERE SUPPOSED TO BE STEALING THE EIFFEL TOWER ON THE DAY IT WAS INAUGURATED!

CAN'T WE REVERSE COURSE AND GO TO PARIS NOW?

NO, DADDY DEAR... THE CATJET ONLY HAS ENOUGH FUEL TO TAKE US BACK TO OUR OWN TIME!

WELL, SINCE WE'RE ALREADY HERE NOW, HOW ABOUT I TAKE A **PHOTO?**

WOULD YOU KNOCK IT OFF, YOU PAIN IN THE TAIL!*

*PAIN IN THE NECK

>GULP!<

SOMEONE'S **ATTACKING US!**

HURRY UP, EVERYBODY ON BOARD! WE'VE GOT TO TAKE OFF AGAIN!

15

YOU JUST GET DUMBER AND DUMBER, BONZO!

WHAT'VE YOU DONE?!

MEOW DOWN*, DADDY DEAR! WE HAVE TO BE CAREFUL ABOUT HOW WE ACT!

A THOUSAND TUMBLING TABBY CATS! CAVE PEOPLE!

*CALM DOWN

DID YOU NOTICE? THEY DON'T LOOK LIKE THEY'RE **AFRAID** OF US!

IT'S PROBABLY BECAUSE THEY'VE NEVER SEEN ANY CATS BEFORE IN THEIR LIVES!

THEY'RE ARMED. WHAT DO WE DO NOW?

TOOLS

NEANDERTHALS HADN'T DISCOVERED IRON AND MADE THEIR TOOLS OUT OF WOOD, BONE, OR STONE. THEY ALSO USED FLINT--A SPECIAL KIND OF ROCK WITH CHARACTERISTICS LIKE GLASS THAT WHEN SPLINTERED OFF, PROVIDED A SHARPENED FOIL THAT WAS USED A GREAT DEAL TO MAKE WEAPONS (KNIVES, SPEARS, AND AXES) AND OTHER TOOLS OF VARIOUS SHAPES AND DIMENSIONS TO WORK WOOD, SCRAPE ANIMAL SKINS, AND CARVE MEAT.

WELL, WE CAN TAKE A BEAUTIFUL PHOTO!

?!?

CLICK

SQUEEEAK!!!

DID YOU SEE THE FLASH OF LIGHTNING?

YES, THE FLASH OF LIGHTNING! I SAW IT!

THEY ARE GODS FROM THE HEAVENS!

BOW DOWN BEFORE THE GODS OF LIGHTNING!

FORGIVE US FOR ATTACKING YOU, OH, POWERFUL GODS! I, RAT-KUN, AND ALL THE RODENTS OF MY TRIBE ARE AT YOUR SERVICE!

POWERFUL GODS? I THOUGHT WE WERE PIRATE CATS!

SILENCE, HAIRBALL!

THE CAVE PEOPLE MISTOOK THE CAMERA FLASH FOR LIGHT-NING!

COME ON! COME WITH ME! I'VE GOT AN IDEA!

BUT...BUT...COME WHERE? AND DO WHAT?

DO WHAT? SIMPLE: PLAY THE ROLE OF GODS! HEE, HEE, HEE!

I GRANT YOU PERMISSION TO GET UP, RAT-KUN!

TH-THANK YOU...

YOU KNOW WE NORMALLY WOULD HAVE ALREADY PUNISHED YOU FOR YOUR ATTACK BY INCINERATING YOU WITH LIGHT-NING!

>GULP!<

BUT WE FEEL GENEROUS TODAY AND HAVE DECIDED TO SPARE YOU!

TH-TH-THANK YOU... AND OUR APOLO-GIES, ONCE AGAIN!

FROM A DISTANCE, SOME OF MY COMPANIONS CONFUSED THE STRANGE ANIMAL YOU TRAVEL ON WITH THE ICE GIANT!

THE ICE GIANT?!?

EXPLAIN THAT TO US, RAT-KUN! WHAT IS THIS MYSTERIOUS ICE GIANT?

IT'S A HUGE, HORRIBLE CREATURE...IT'S FIVE TIMES BIGGER THAN A MAMMOTH AND HAS ENORMOUS TUSKS!

THE MAMMOTH

THE MAMMOTH IS A SPECIES OF ELEPHANT THAT LIVED FROM ABOUT 5,000,000 TO 6,000 YEARS AGO IN EUROPE, AFRICA, AND NORTH AMERICA. COMPARED TO TODAY'S ELEPHANTS, MAMMOTHS HAD LONG, CURVED TUSKS AND THICK FUR ALL OVER THEIR BODIES. THEY AVERAGED AROUND 9.2 FEET TALL AND COULD REACH 14.7 FEET IN LENGTH. LIKE TODAY'S ELEPHANTS, MAMMOTHS WERE HERBIVORES.

IN THE PAST FEW DAYS, THE RODENTS OF MY TRIBE HAVE OFTEN HEARD **FEARSOME WAILS...**

"...THAT CAME FROM THE LARGE ICE SHEET. AND WHEN THEY APPROACHED IT, THEY SAW A HORRIBLE MONSTER!"

NOW WE'RE SO SCARED WE DON'T DARE VENTURE OVER THERE ANYMORE!

HMM...VERY INTERESTING...

DID YOU HEAR THAT? MAYBE OUR TRIP WASN'T A TOTAL WASTE!

WHAT DO YOU MEAN, TERSILLA?

IF WE MANAGE TO CAPTURE THE ICE GIANT AND BRING IT BACK TO CATBURG WITH US, WE'LL BE FAMOUS!

YOU WANT...TO CAPTURE THAT monster?!?

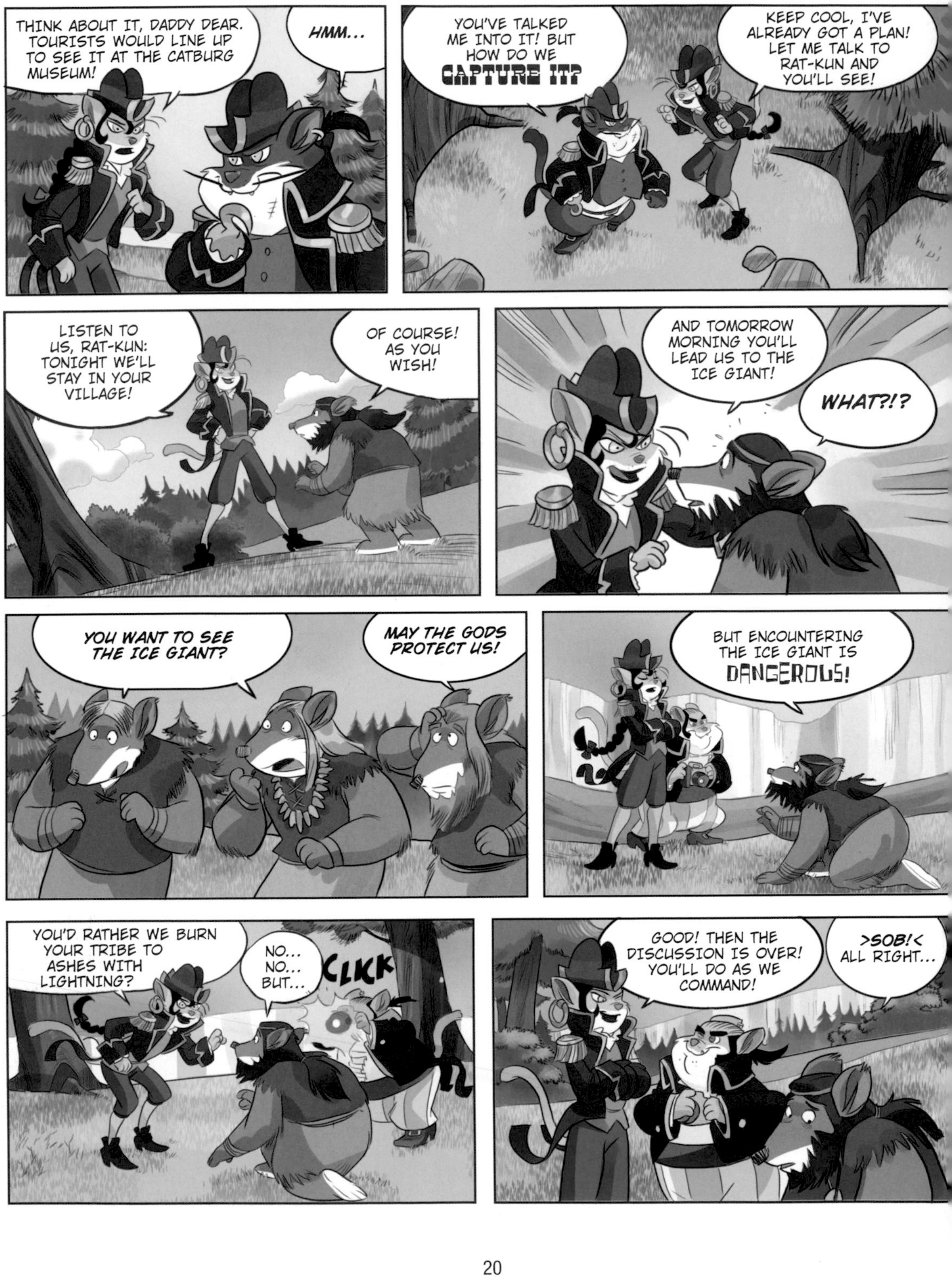
THINK ABOUT IT, DADDY DEAR. TOURISTS WOULD LINE UP TO SEE IT AT THE CATBURG MUSEUM!
HMM...
YOU'VE TALKED ME INTO IT! BUT HOW DO WE CAPTURE IT?
KEEP COOL, I'VE ALREADY GOT A PLAN! LET ME TALK TO RAT-KUN AND YOU'LL SEE!
LISTEN TO US, RAT-KUN: TONIGHT WE'LL STAY IN YOUR VILLAGE!
OF COURSE! AS YOU WISH!
AND TOMORROW MORNING YOU'LL LEAD US TO THE ICE GIANT!
WHAT?!?
YOU WANT TO SEE THE ICE GIANT?
MAY THE GODS PROTECT US!
BUT ENCOUNTERING THE ICE GIANT IS DANGEROUS!
YOU'D RATHER WE BURN YOUR TRIBE TO ASHES WITH LIGHTNING?
NO... NO... BUT...
CLICK
GOOD! THEN THE DISCUSSION IS OVER! YOU'LL DO AS WE COMMAND!
>SOB!< ALL RIGHT...

MEANWHILE, WE'D LANDED THE SPEEDRAT RIGHT ON THE ICE SHEET...

BRRR... IT'S COLD AS A CAT'S HEART.

WELL, WE'RE RIGHT IN THE MIDDLE OF THE **WURM GLACIATION!**

THE WURM GLACIATION

WAS THE LAST BIG GLACIATION TO AFFECT THE EARTH. IT LASTED FROM AROUND 80,000 TO 11,000 YEARS AGO AND GETS ITS NAME FROM A RIVER IN THE REGION OF BAVARIA, IN GERMANY. IT'S ALSO KNOWN AS THE WISCONSIN (FROM THE NAME OF THE STATE IN NORTH AMERICA) OR WEICHSEL GLACIATION (THE NAME OF A REGION IN NORTHERN EUROPE).

I KNOW, BUT I WONDER HOW ICE AGE CAVE PEOPLE KEPT FROM FREEZING **DRESSED** LIKE THIS!

CLOTHES

NEANDERTHALS WERE PROBABLY THE FIRST HUMAN BEINGS WHO REGULARLY WORE CLOTHING TO PROTECT THEMSELVES FROM THE COLD. THEIR CLOTHING WAS MADE FROM THE SKINS AND FURS OF VARIOUS ANIMALS, WHICH, AFTER BEING STRETCHED AND SCRAPED WITH FLINT TOOLS, WERE SEWN INTO CLOTHING AND SHOES. NEANDERTHALS MADE NECKLACES AND BRACELETS FROM ANIMAL TEETH TO WEAR AS JEWELRY.

NOW WE CAN GO! HEY, WAIT A MINUTE...TRAP, WHAT ARE YOU DOING HERE WITH THAT GOLF BAG?

TO STAY ON TOP OF HIS GAME, A CHAMPION MUST NEVER STOP TRAINING!

BUT GOLF HADN'T BEEN INVENTED YET IN THIS ERA! YOU CAN'T CARRY GOLF EQUIPMENT!

COME ON, COUSIN, I PROMISE I'LL ONLY PLAY AFTER THE MISSION IS ACCOMPLISHED!

ALL RIGHT, ALL RIGHT...IT'S USELESS TO ARGUE ABOUT IT!

BUT WHERE SHOULD WE START LOOKING FOR THE PIRATE CATS?

THERE'S ONLY **ICE** AROUND HERE!

THE ICE SHEET SEEMS TO END OVER THERE! LET'S TRY TO TAKE A LOOK!

LOOK! THERE'S A FOREST OVER THERE! WHAT A *RAT-TASTIC* VIEW!

YOU'RE A REGULAR ROMAN-TIC, COUSIN!

PAFF

SQUEEEAK!

I'M FALLINGGGGGGG!

TUMF

22

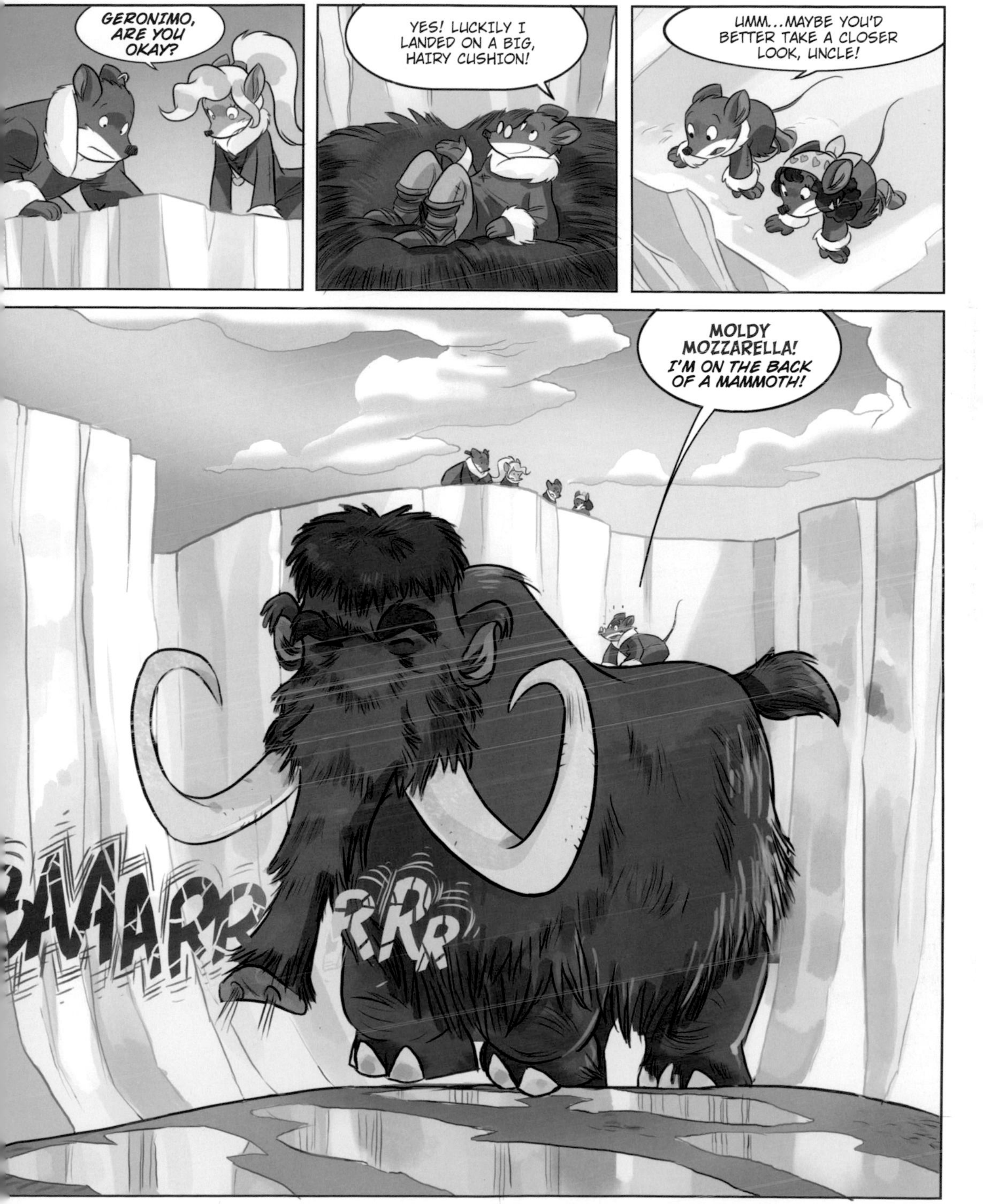
GERONIMO, ARE YOU OKAY?
YES! LUCKILY I LANDED ON A BIG, HAIRY CUSHION!
UMM...MAYBE YOU'D BETTER TAKE A CLOSER LOOK, UNCLE!
MOLDY MOZZARELLA! I'M ON THE BACK OF A MAMMOTH!

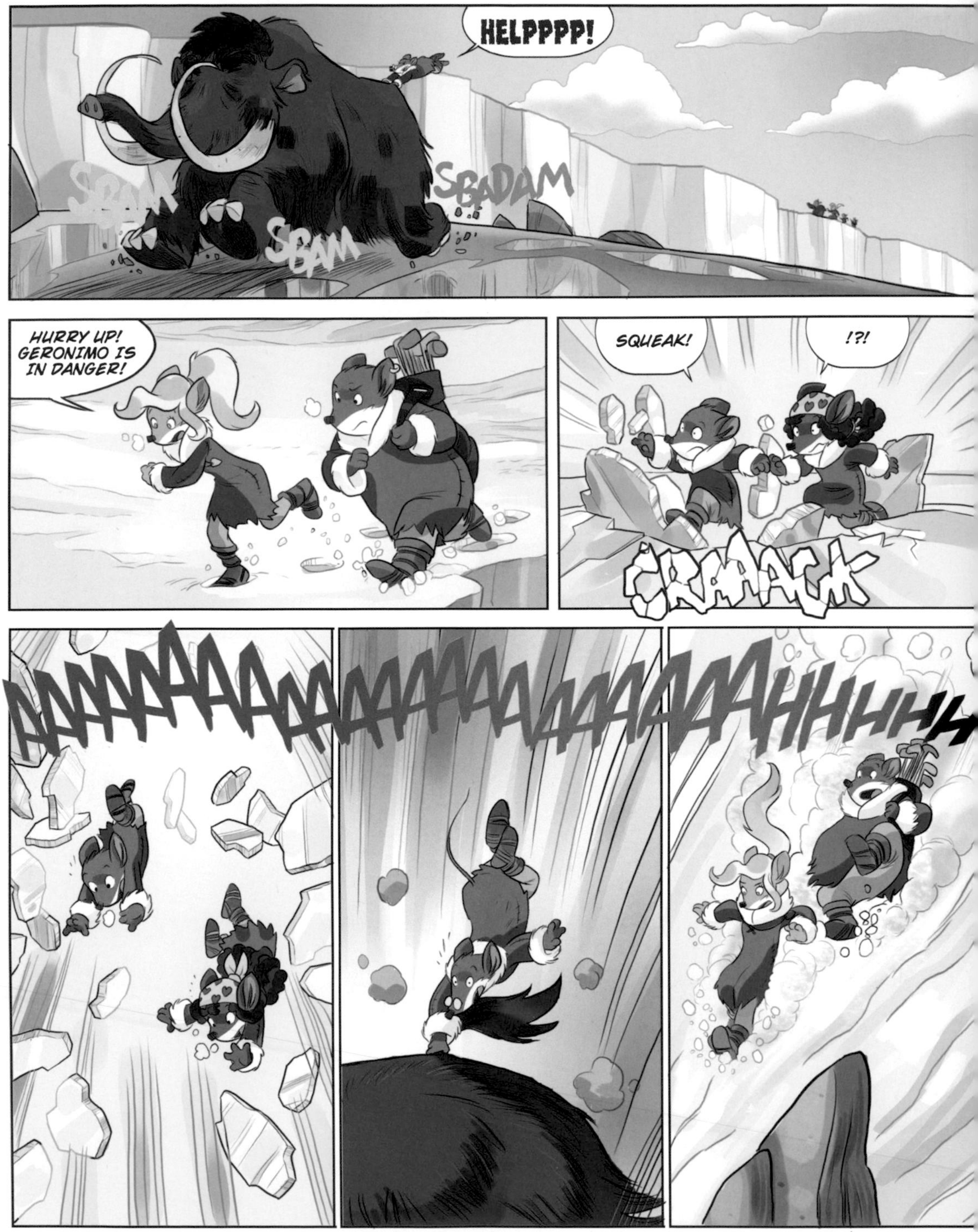
HELPPPP!
SBAM
SBADAM
SBAM
HURRY UP! GERONIMO IS IN DANGER!
SQUEAK!
!?!
CRAAACK
AAAAAAAAAAAAAAAAAAAAAAAAAAAHHHHH

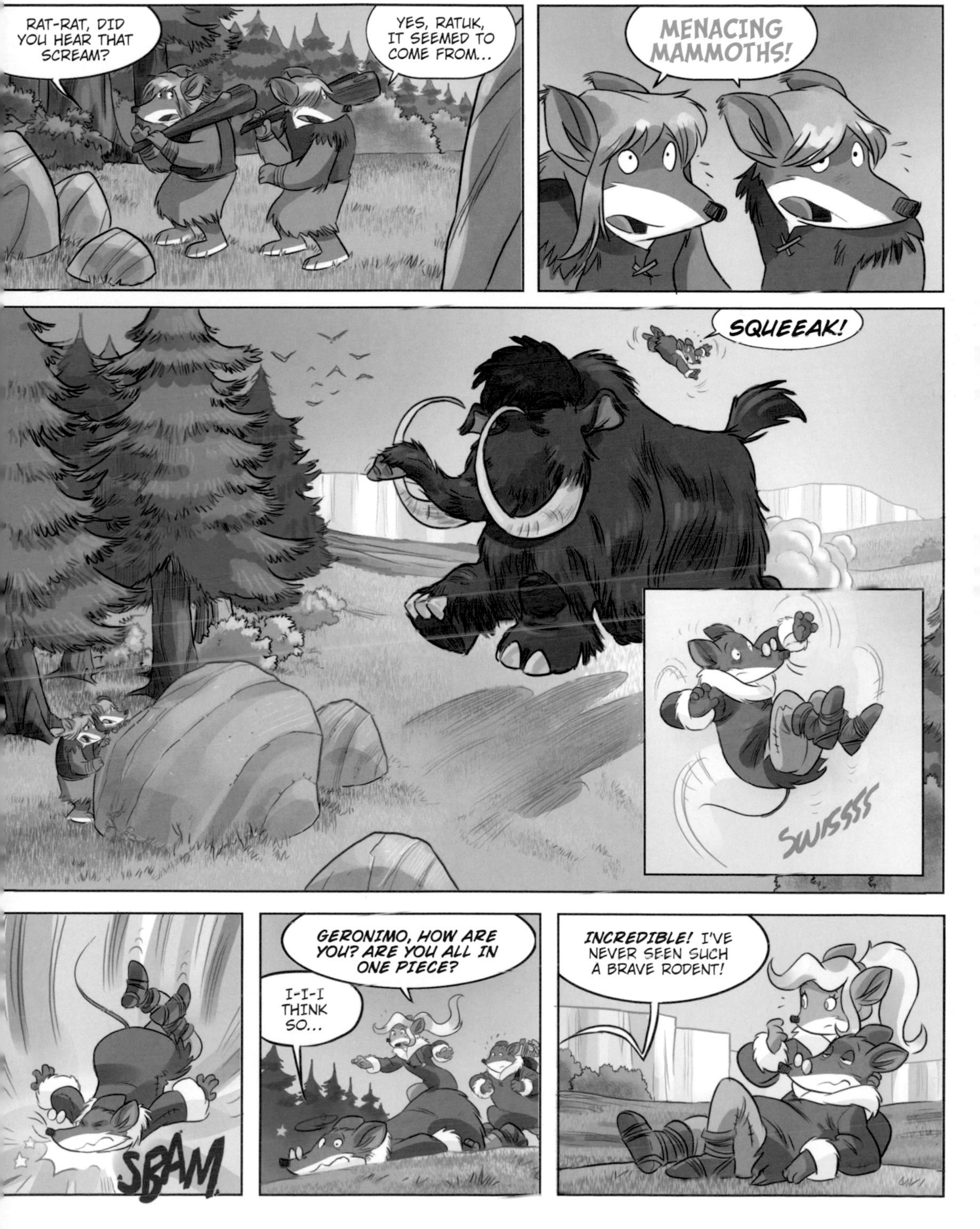
RAT-RAT, DID YOU HEAR THAT SCREAM?
YES, RATUK, IT SEEMED TO COME FROM...
MENACING MAMMOTHS!
SQUEEAK!
SWISSSS
SBAM
GERONIMO, HOW ARE YOU? ARE YOU ALL IN ONE PIECE?
I-I-I THINK SO...
INCREDIBLE! I'VE NEVER SEEN SUCH A BRAVE RODENT!

NO ONE IN OUR TRIBE WOULD HAVE EVER DARED TO FACE THAT MAMMOTH!

THEY ALL KNOW IT'S A VERY FEROCIOUS BEAST!

WH-WH-WHAT? DID YOU SAY FEROCIOUS?

IN THE LAST FEW DAYS, IT'S GONE AFTER ANYBODY WHO CAME NEAR IT...WHEN IT WASN'T EVEN BEING ATTACKED!

I THINK IT'S EVEN SCARIER THAN THE ICE GIANT!

WHAT ARE YOU TALKING ABOUT? THIS IS JUST A MAMMOTH, WHILE THE ICE GIANT...

...IS A REAL MONSTER!

I THINK THE MAMMOTH IS MUCH WORSE!

NO WAY!

UM... EXCUSE ME?

EXCUSE ME FOR BUTTING IN, BUT...COULD YOU TELL US WHO YOU ARE?

OH, YEAH, SORRY! MY NAME IS RAT-RAT...

...AND I'M RATUK! WE'RE THE CHILDREN OF THE GREAT TRIBAL LEADER RAT-KUN!

PLEASED TO MEET YOU! MY NAME IS STILTONUT, GERONIMUT STILTONUT. THIS IS MY FRIEND PATTUT, MY COUSIN TRAPPUT, MY NEPHEW, BEN--!

BUT... WHERE...?

MOLDY MOZZARELLA! WHAT HAPPENED TO BENJAMUT AND PANDORUT?

I DON'T UNDER-STAND...THEY WERE RIGHT BEHIND US!

THAT'S RIGHT! HOW DID THEY GET LOST?

IF THEY GOT LOST, IT WON'T BE EASY TO FIND THEM: THE REGION IS HUGE!

BUT WE HAVE TO FIND THEM!

COME TO THE VILLAGE! WE'LL GET ALL THE RODENTS TOGETHER AND SEARCH THE GRASSLANDS!

BUT...

RATUK AND RAT-RAT ARE RIGHT! WE DON'T KNOW THE AREA AND WE'LL RISK GETTING OURSELVES LOST, TOO!

THAT'S TRUE...LET'S GO!

CHEER UP, GERONIMO! I'M SURE...

"...THAT BENJAMIN AND PANDORA ARE OKAY!"

A LITTLE LATER, WE ARRIVED IN A GENUINE PRIMITIVE VILLAGE...

>SLURP!< THIS LOOKS GREAT!

GET A MOVE ON, TRAPPUT!

DWELLINGS

NEANDERTHALS LIVED IN CAVES OR CAMPS OUTDOORS, WHERE THEY BUILT HUTS OUT OF ANIMAL SKINS STRETCHED OVER A PANELWORK OF STAKES OR MAMMOTH BONES. TO WARM UP, KEEP WILD ANIMALS AWAY, AND COOK, THEY USED FIRE, WHICH THEY LIT BY RUBBING TWO STONES OR STICKS TOGETHER.

28

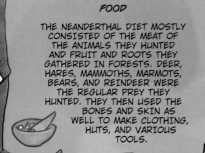

FOOD

THE NEANDERTHAL DIET MOSTLY CONSISTED OF THE MEAT OF THE ANIMALS THEY HUNTED AND FRUIT AND ROOTS THEY GATHERED IN FORESTS. DEER, HARES, MAMMOTHS, MARMOTS, BEARS, AND REINDEER WERE THE REGULAR PREY THEY HUNTED. THEY THEN USED THE BONES AND SKIN AS WELL TO MAKE CLOTHING, HUTS, AND VARIOUS TOOLS.

YOUR **TRIBE** SEEMS VERY BUSY!

OH, YES! THIS EVENING WE'RE HOSTING A BIG BANQUET IN HONOR OF THREE POWERFUL GODS WHO ARRIVED TODAY!

THREE GODS?

UM...DO YOU SMELL THE STINK OF THE PIRATE CATS, TOO?

THE P-P-PIRATE CATS!

THAT'S RIGHT! WITH BENJAMIN AND PANDORA DISAPPEARING, I ALMOST FORGOT ABOUT THEM!

OUR FATHER'S OVER THERE: HE'S WITH THE GODS!

UH-OH! I SINCERELY HOPE THEY AREN'T...

...THE PIRATE CATS!!!

GERONIMO STILTON AND HIS FRIENDS?

RAT-KUN, I COMMAND YOU TO IMPRISON THOSE RODENTS IMMEDIATELY!

IMPRISON THEM? WHY?

DO YOU DARE CHALLENGE A DIVINE ORDER, MOUSE?

NO...NO... REALLY...

BUT, FATHER, THESE RODENTS HAVEN'T DONE ANYTHING WRONG! THEY'RE HERE BECAUSE THEY NEED OUR **HELP!**

I CAN'T DO ANYTHING ABOUT IT, RATUK... YOU HEARD THE GODS, TOO! THEY'VE CHOSEN THIS...

LISTEN TO US: THEY AREN'T GODS, THEY'RE FAKERS!

WE KNOW THEM WELL!

HOW DARE YOU, MICE!

RAT-KUN, WHAT ARE YOU WAITING FOR? I ORDERED YOU TO IMPRISON THEM!

SWOOOM

OH, OH! MY **HEAD...** WHAT BAD MANNERS!

I BEG YOU TO FREE US! OUR NIECE AND NEPHEW ARE IN GRAVE DANGER...AND SO ARE YOU!

SORRY, GERONIMUT, BUT WE CAN'T DISOBEY THE GODS...FOR THE SAKE OF OUR FUR!

HOW CAN WE GET IT ACROSS TO YOU...THOSE AREN'T GODS! THEY'RE CATS AND THEY'RE SCOUNDRELS!

IT'S A WASTE OF BREATH, GERONIMO! THEY'LL NEVER BELIEVE US.

YOU'RE RIGHT. BUT ISN'T THERE SOMETHING WE CAN DO?

FOR NOW, WE CAN JUST STAY CALM AND WAIT FOR THE RIGHT OPPORTUNITY TO ESCAPE.

WHILE WE'RE WAITING, I HOPE THEY GIVE US SOMETHING TO EAT AT LEAST: I'M HUNGRY AS A FELINE!

>SIGH!<

THAT NIGHT, A BIG BANQUET WAS HELD IN HONOR OF THE PIRATE CATS.

31

WE GOT TO SLEEP LATE THAT NIGHT AND AT DAWN...

ZZZZZZZ

SQUEEEAK!

SPLASH

WAKE UP, MICE, IT'S TIME TO GO!

GO? WITH YOU? WHERE TO?

WE'RE ALL LEAVING TO HUNT THE ICE GIANT!

THAT'S THE MONSTROUS CREATURE THAT RATUK WAS TALKING ABOUT! SO IS THAT YOUR GOAL?

RIGHT! WE'RE GOING TO TAKE IT TO CATBURG WITH US AND YOU CAN'T DO ANYTHING TO STOP US!

AS A MATTER OF FACT, YOUR FATE HAS BEEN SETTLED: WE'VE ORDERED RAT-KUN TO SACRIFICE YOU TO THE ICE GIANT BY THROWING YOU INTO A CHASM... HEE, HEE, HEE!

32

>GULP<! WHAT A HORRIBLE END!

WHAT A CHEESEHEAD!

HAVE YOU PUT EVERYTHING ONTO THE CATJET WE'LL NEED TO CAPTURE THE MONSTER?

OF COURSE, TERSILLA! I'VE GOT THE BLOW-TORCH...

...AND THE STEEL CABLES WE WERE GOING TO USE TO STEAL THE EIFFEL TOWER!

PERFECT...LET'S GET GOING!

THE EXPEDITION WENT ACROSS THE GRASS LANDS, HEADING FOR THE ICE GIANT...

STOP!

THE GREAT ICE SHEET IS PAST THESE TREES!

IT WOULD BE BETTER TO LEAVE THE CAGE WITH THE PRISONERS HERE! IF THE GIANT ATTACKS US, IT WILL GET IN OUR WAY!

AGREED. IN THAT CASE, LET'S SACRIFICE THE PRISONERS WHEN WE GET BACK!

FOUR RODENTS FROM MY TRIBE WILL STAY TO KEEP GUARD OVER THEM!

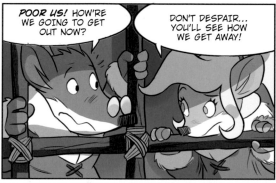

POOR US! HOW'RE WE GOING TO GET OUT NOW?

DON'T DESPAIR... YOU'LL SEE HOW WE GET AWAY!

I WISH I WERE AS HOPEFUL AS PATTY!

THE CATS WERE ABSOLUTELY DETER-MINED TO CARRY OUT THEIR PLAN...

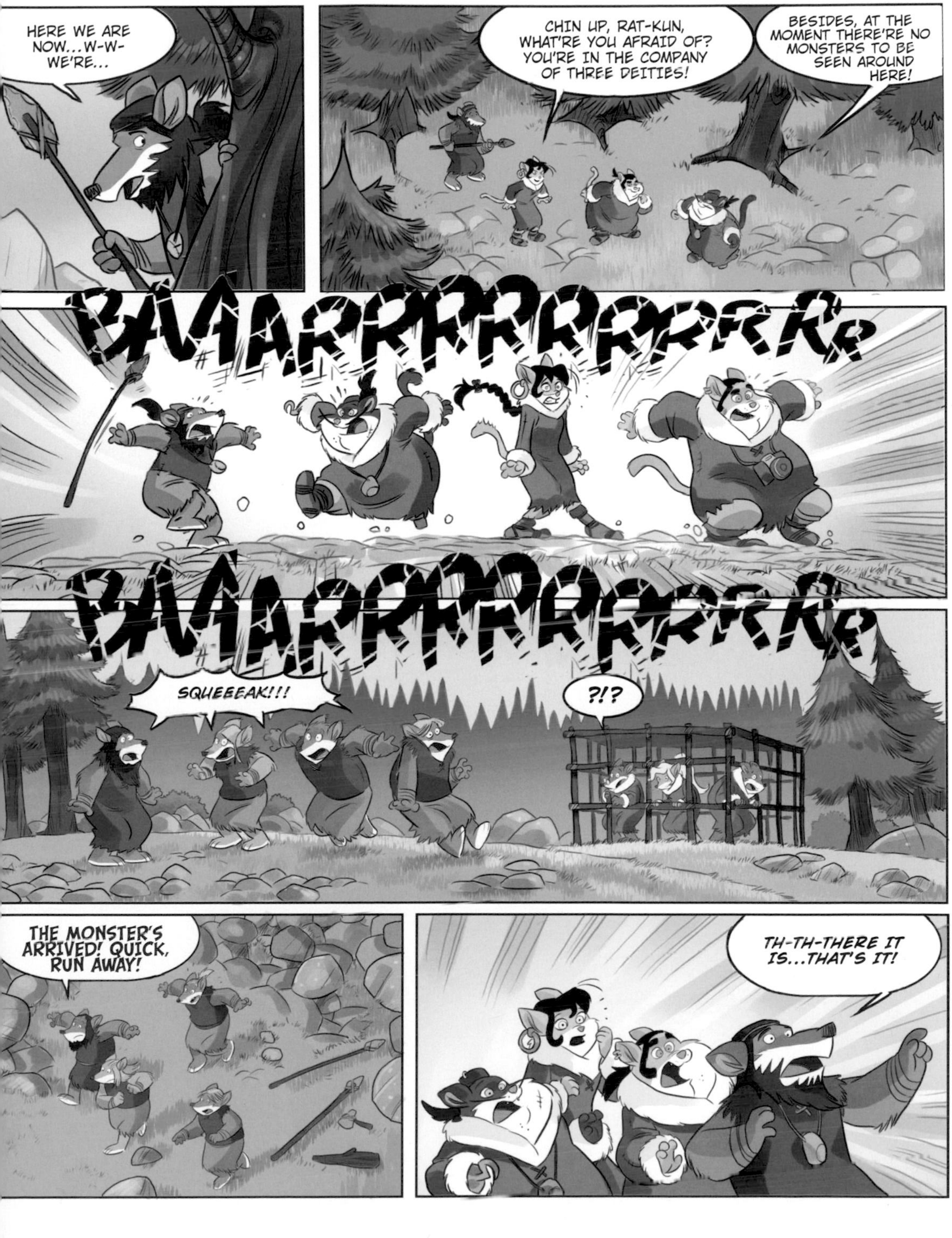
HERE WE ARE NOW...W-W-WE'RE...
CHIN UP, RAT-KUN, WHAT'RE YOU AFRAID OF? YOU'RE IN THE COMPANY OF THREE DEITIES!
BESIDES, AT THE MOMENT THERE'RE NO MONSTERS TO BE SEEN AROUND HERE!
BWAARRRRRRRRRRR
BWAARRRRRRRRRRR
SQUEEEAK!!!
?!?
THE MONSTER'S ARRIVED! QUICK, RUN AWAY!
TH-TH-THERE IT IS...THAT'S IT!

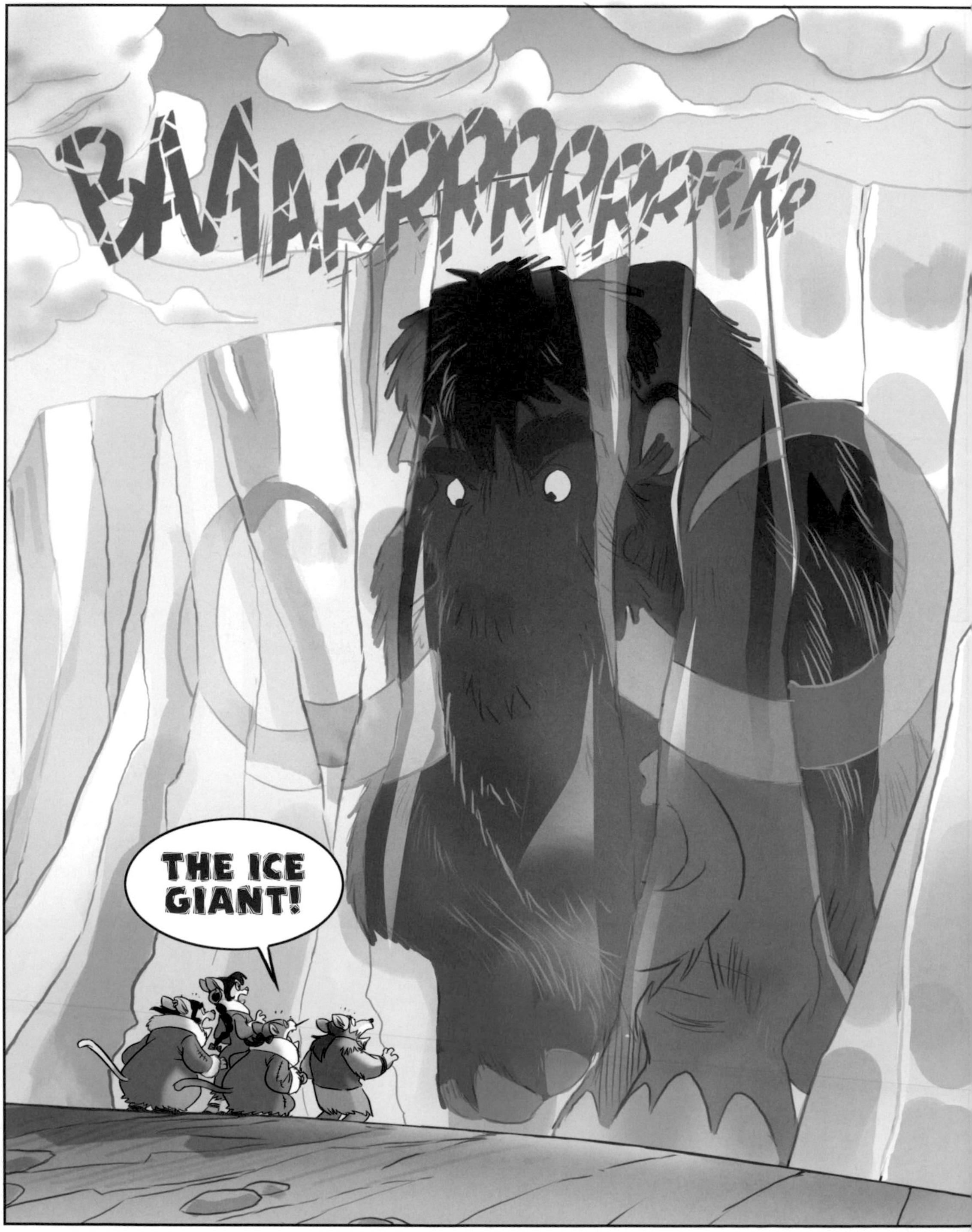
BAAARRRRRRRRRRRR
THE ICE GIANT!

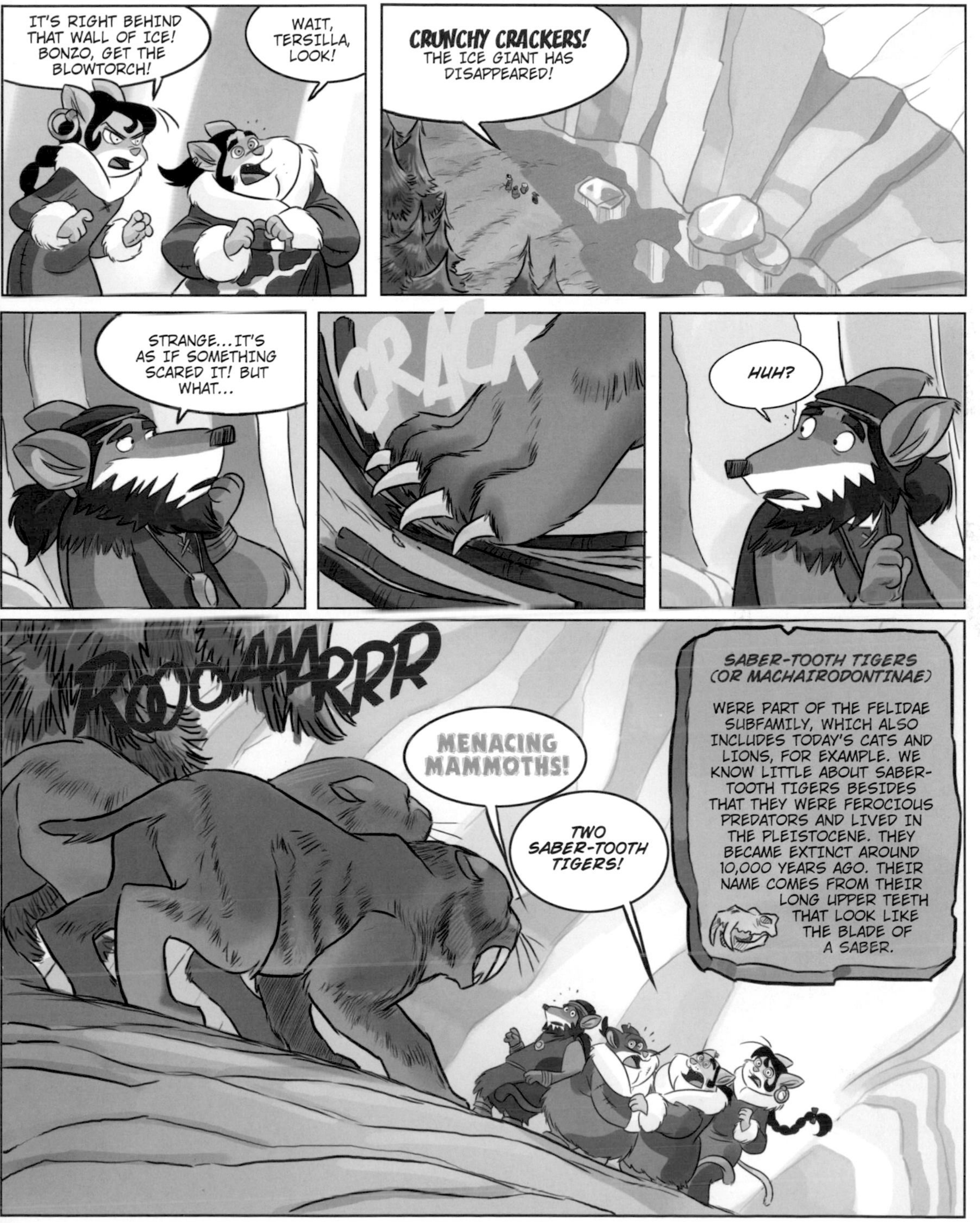

IT'S RIGHT BEHIND THAT WALL OF ICE! BONZO, GET THE BLOWTORCH!
WAIT, TERSILLA, LOOK!
CRUNCHY CRACKERS! THE ICE GIANT HAS DISAPPEARED!
STRANGE...IT'S AS IF SOMETHING SCARED IT! BUT WHAT...
CRACK
HUH?
ROOOAAARRRR
MENACING MAMMOTHS!
TWO SABER-TOOTH TIGERS!
SABER-TOOTH TIGERS (OR MACHAIRODONTINAE)
WERE PART OF THE FELIDAE SUBFAMILY, WHICH ALSO INCLUDES TODAY'S CATS AND LIONS, FOR EXAMPLE. WE KNOW LITTLE ABOUT SABER-TOOTH TIGERS BESIDES THAT THEY WERE FEROCIOUS PREDATORS AND LIVED IN THE PLEISTOCENE. THEY BECAME EXTINCT AROUND 10,000 YEARS AGO. THEIR NAME COMES FROM THEIR LONG UPPER TEETH THAT LOOK LIKE THE BLADE OF A SABER.

QUICK, LET'S CLIMB UP THIS TREE!

GGRRRR

I BESEECH YOU, POWERFUL GODS, USE YOUR **BLINDING FLASH** OF LIGHTNING OR THE TIGERS WILL DEVOUR US!

RIGHT! BONZO, YOU CAN USE THE FLASH TO DISORIENT THEM WHILE WE ESCAPE!

Y-Y-YES, TERSILLA... I'LL GET MY CAMERA AND...

...OOPS!

CRASH

UM...I GUESS WE'LL HAVE TO WAIT UP HERE!

GRRRR!

AT THAT VERY SAME MOMENT, IN A FOREST NOT TOO FAR AWAY...

>NNNNG<...IF I COULD ONLY MANAGE TO GET HOLD OF THAT AXE, I COULD USE IT TO BREAK THE BARS OF THIS CAGE!

FRUSH FRUSH

WAIT! WE'LL HELP YOU, UNCLE GERONIMO!

???

MOLDY MOZZARELLA! BENJAMIN! PANDORA! YOU'RE SAFE!

YES, WE'RE FINE! WE'LL GET YOU OUT IN A MINUTE! BUT WHAT ARE YOU DOING HERE?

FEAK

IT WAS THE PIRATE CATS...OH, BENJAMIN, PANDORA! I'M SO HAPPY TO SEE YOU! WE WERE SO WORRIED!

39

BUT WHERE DID YOU DISAPPEAR TO?

RIGHT, WHERE'VE YOU BEEN? AND IN PARTICULAR, HOW DID YOU FIND US?

OH, FINDING YOU WAS EASY...WE WERE JUST LEAVING THIS FOREST WHEN WE SAW PRISONERS IN A CAGE...

AS FOR WHERE WE'VE BEEN...IT ALL HAPPENED WHEN UNCLE GERONIMO WAS ON THE BACK OF THE **MAMMOTH!**

"BENJAMIN AND I WERE RUNNING TO HELP HIM WHEN WE FELL INTO A CHASM..."

CRAAACK-

"AS SOON AS WE RECOVERED FROM OUR FALL, WE DISCOVERED WE WERE INSIDE A TUNNEL UNDER THE ICE SHEET!"

"WE WALKED FOR HOURS LOOKING FOR A WAY OUT AND IN THE END WE ARRIVED NEAR HERE..."

"...IN FRONT OF A BIG WALL OF ICE, ACROSS FROM WHICH WE SAW THE FOREST!"

"IT WAS THEN WE REALIZED WE WEREN'T ALONE... SOMEONE ELSE WAS TRAPPED IN THE ICE TUNNEL WITH US!"

Y-YOU DIDN'T MEET THAT MONSTER... THE ICE GIANT?

NO, UNCLE, IT'S NOT A **MONSTER!**

IN FACT, YOU, AUNT PATTY, AND TRAP ABSOLUTELY MUST COME WITH US TO HELP IT.

YES, BUT...WE CAN'T RIGHT NOW: WE HAVE TO STOP THE PIRATE CATS!

UNCLE...PLEASE! IT'S REALLY **IMPORTANT!**

COME ON, GERONIMO! FOLLOW US QUICKLY!

HEY, KIDS! WHERE'RE YOU GOING? WAIT FOR US!

A LITTLE LATER...

THIS IS THE HOLE PANDORA AND I CAME OUT OF!

41

?!?

ROLLICKING RATS! THERE'S A BABY MAMMOTH DOWN THERE!

A BABY MAMMOTH?

WHY DIDN'T YOU SAY SO IMMEDIATELY?

WE WANTED IT TO BE A SURPRISE!

BUT WHAT IS A BABY MAMMOTH DOING HERE? HE SEEMS TO BE TRAPPED!

YES! PLUS, WE'RE RIGHT IN THAT MONSTER'S TERRITORY...THE ICE GIANT...I DON'T WANT TO RUN INTO IT!

WE NEED SHOVELS TO ENLARGE THE HOLE AND ROPE TO PULL OUT THE BABY MAMMOTH!

I HEARD THE PIRATE CATS HAVE A BLOWTORCH AND STEEL CABLES!

YOU'RE NOT THINKING OF ASKING THOSE SCOUNDRELS FOR HELP!?! AND BESIDES, WHO KNOWS WHERE THEY ARE?

ACTUALLY... THEY'RE CLOSER THAN YOU THINK, COUSIN!

?!?

LOOK! RAT-KLIN AND THE PIRATE CATS ARE IN DANGER!

EVEN IF THEY DON'T DESERVE IT, WE HAVE TO HELP THEM AND GET THOSE TIGERS AWAY FROM THEM!

RIGHT! BUT WHAT CAN WE DO?

WELL...WHAT DO YOU SAY TO A GAME OF GOLF?

WHAT'S GOLF GOT TO DO WITH IT?

I HAVE A RAT-TASTIC PLAN IN MIND: YOU'LL UNDERSTAND IT QUICKLY...BUT FIRST WE HAVE TO GET SOME **SNOWBALLS** READY!

HMM...WHAT COULD TRAP HAVE IN MIND? >MUMBLE... MUMBLE...<

BUT, OF COURSE! I GET IT! WHAT A RAT-TASTIC IDEA, TRAP!

SO...

ARE YOU READY?

I'M QUITE READY!

TRY NOT TO **HIT** ME THIS TIME!

SLAM
SLAM
SLAM

SPLAFF

SPLAFF

SPLAFF

BUT...BUT...SOMEONE'S BOMBARDING THE TIGERS!

WHO COULD IT BE?

HMM...I HAVE A REALLY BAD FEELING...

HEY LOOK!

THE TIGERS ARE RUNNING AWAY! WE FINALLY CAN GET DOWN!

>SOB!< MY CAMERA'S COMPLETELY DESTROYED!

RIGHT...AND WITHOUT THAT CAMERA WE CAN'T MAKE RAT-KUN BELIEVE WE'RE GODS!

?!?

STOP RIGHT THERE, YOU CRUMMY CATS!

THE PRISONERS... MANAGED TO GET FREE!!!

YES, LUCKILY FOR YOU, RAT-KUN,... SEEING WE'RE THE ONES WHO CHASED THE TIGERS AWAY!

I...I DON'T KNOW HOW TO THANK YOU!

OH, BELIEVE ME...THERE'LL BE A WAY!

!?

I HAVE A HUNCH WE'D BETTER ESCAPE IN A HURRY, DADDY DEAR!

BUT...THE ICE GIANT? WE'RE GOING TO LEAVE IT HERE?

SINCE WE DON'T HAVE THE CAMERA, STILTON CAN CONVINCE RAT-KUN WE AREN'T GODS AND WE'LL BE IN HOT WATER!

>GULP!<

LET'S GET OUT OF HERE!

FSHOOOM

I DON'T UNDERSTAND...WHAT HAPPENED? WHY DID THE GODS LEAVE?

I'LL EXPLAIN EVERYTHING, RAT-KUN... BUT FIRST YOU HAVE TO HELP US RESCUE A FRIEND!

I QUICKLY TOLD THE TRIBE'S LEADER ABOUT THE BABY MAMMOTH TRAPPED IN THE ICE...

>SQUEAK!< BUT THAT'S WHERE WE SAW THE ICE GIANT!

YOU KNOW, I'M BEGINNING TO SUSPECT THAT THE ICE GIANT DOESN'T ACTUALLY EXIST...

IF IT DOESN'T EXIST... WH-WH-WHAT'S THAT?

RAAARRRROARRR

MOLDY MOZZARELLA!

HELP! RUN FOR IT!

?!?

I'D BETTER RACE AFTER RAT-KUN AND BRING HIM BACK!

OKAY, IN THE MEANTIME, I'M GOING TO TRY TO CLEAR UP THIS MYSTERY! HELP ME, TRAP!

A LITTLE LATER, WHILE I CAUGHT UP WITH RAT-KUN AND TRIED TO EXPLAIN EVERYTHING AND CALM HIM DOWN, PATTY AND TRAP GOT THE PIRATE CATS' BLOWTORCH AND PUT IT TO WORK...

FZZZZZ

AND WHEN WE GOT BACK, TRAP HAD ALREADY MANAGED TO MELT THE ICE AND OPEN UP A GAP...

GERONIMO, RAT-KUN, COME HERE! I'D LIKE TO PRESENT TO YOU... *THE ICE BABY!*

MENACING *MAMMOTHS!*

BUT...BUT...WHERE DID HE COME FROM? AND WHAT'S HE GOT TO DO WITH THE MONSTER?

HE JUST CAME FROM THAT ICE TUNNEL...THE MONSTER WAS HIM!

HE LOOKED LIKE A MONSTER DUE TO A STRANGE OPTICAL EFFECT OF THE ICE THAT CHANGED HIS APPEARANCE!

WHEREAS THE TRUMPETING SOUNDED SO SCARY BECAUSE IT BOOMED UNDER THE ICE SHEET!

EVERYTHING'S CLEAR NOW, BUT WHO KNOWS HOW THE BABY MAMMOTH WOUND UP OVER THERE...

HE PROBABLY GOT SEPARATED FROM HIS MOTHER AND FELL INTO A CHASM BY MISTAKE!

HEE, HEE, HEE...HE'S SO **FRIENDLY!**

AS FOR HIS MOTHER...I WONDER WHERE SHE COULD HAVE ENDED UP? MAYBE SHE'S LOOKING FOR...

SQUEEEAK! WHAT'S THAT?!?

BBAAARRR

47

CALAMITOUS CATS! THAT'S THE REALLY FEROCIOUS MAMMOTH I LANDED ON!

BBBAADRRRR

?!?

BUT OF COURSE! THAT MAMMOTH HAS TO BE HIS MAMA!

THAT'S PROBABLY WHY SHE WAS SO FURIOUS: SHE COULDN'T FIND HER BABY!

AND NOW THEY'RE FINALLY BACK TOGETHER AGAIN... >SNIFF<... I ALWAYS FIND THESE SCENES SO TOUCHING!

YOU'RE A REGULAR ROMANTIC, COUSIN! BUT THAT'S ENOUGH BLUBBERING NOW!

PAFF

THE MAMMOTHS SAID GOODBYE TO US... IN THEIR OWN WAY!

BBBAADRRR

48

WELL, WE'VE COME TO THE END OF OUR ADVENTURE! ONCE AGAIN, WE'VE FOILED THE PIRATE CATS' PLANS!

YOU'VE WON AGAIN, STILTON! BUT DON'T DELUDE YOURSELF, SOONER OR LATER, WE'LL GET OUR REVENGE!

TO THANK US FOR HAVING SAVED THEM FROM THE TIGERS AND SOLVING THE MYSTERY OF THE ICE GIANT, RAT-KUN ARRANGED A BIG PARTY...

I'M GLAD YOU FOUND YOUR FRIENDS AGAIN!

SORRY WE DOUBTED YOU!

AFTER THE PARTY, WE SAID GOODBYE TO RAT-KUN, RATUK, AND RAT-RAT AND HEADED FOR THE SPEEDRAT. WE HAD TO GET BACK TO NEW MOUSE CITY!

PLEASE ACCEPT THIS NECKLACE AS A THANK YOU GIFT!

THANKS, EVERYONE!

JEWELRY

CAVE PEOPLE WORE VARIOUS TYPES OF NECKLACES AND BRACELETS. THIS JEWELRY WAS MADE OF SEA SHELLS, SMALL COLORED STONES, DRIED INSECTS, AND, ESPECIALLY, THE TEETH AND CLAWS OF WILD ANIMALS (BEARS, TIGERS, AND WOLVES), THAT HUNTERS EXHIBITED AS THEIR OWN, AUTHENTIC TROPHIES AS PROOF OF THEIR COURAGE.

ONCE AGAIN THIS TIME, PROF. VOLT WAS WAITING FOR US IN HIS LAB...

WELCOME BACK, MY FRIENDS! WAS YOUR TRIP A SUCCESS?

YES, PROFESSOR, EVEN THOUGH IT WAS MORE COMPLICATED AND ADVENTUROUS THAN USUAL!

WHEN WE TELL YOU WHAT THE PIRATE CAT'S GOAL WAS, YOU WON'T BELIEVE YOUR EARS!

I CAN'T WAIT TO HEAR THE WHOLE STORY...BUT FIRST, LET'S CELEBRATE!

WITH GREAT PLEASURE, PROFESS... >SQUEEEAK!<

STOCK

OOPS...SORRY, COUSIN! YOU TOLD ME WHEN THE MISSION WAS OVER I COULD START TRAINING AGAIN!

MY POOR HEAD! THAT HURTS!

MY DEAR RODENT FRIENDS, FAREWELL UNTIL THE NEXT ADVEN- TURE... ANOTHER WHISKERFUL OF AN ADVENTURE, WRITTEN BY STILTON...GERONIMO STILTON!

HA, HA, HA!

Watch Out For
PAPERCUTZ

Something funny was going on in an office on the thirteenth floor in an office building on Manhattan Island. Michael Petranek, Papercutz editorial assistant, was having a crisis. Hold on, I forgot to introduce myself. My name is Salicrup, *Jim Salicrup*, and I'm the Editor-in-Chief at Papercutz, the most famous kids graphic novel publisher on Exchange Place. Michael just received from our printer brand new copies of both the latest GERONIMO STILTON graphic novel and new DISNEY FAIRIES graphic novel, and he didn't know which one to look at first.

On one hand, Michael loved the great, big, adventure story featured in each GERONIMO STILTON graphic novel, but on the other hand, it was also fun to have several shorter stories collected in one DISNEY FAIRIES graphic novel. Similarly, Michael always enjoys the time-travel and historic references found in every GERONIMO STILTON graphic novel, yet he also loves the fantasy-filled fun found in Pixie Hollow, where Tinker Bell and her fairy friends live in Never Land as shown in every DISNEY FAIRIES graphic novel. Furthermore, Michael also liked to see Geronimo foil the latest schemes of the Pirate Cats, but he also knew that Captain Hook and his pirates were always lurking about in Never Land ready to cause trouble! Michael just didn't know what to do. Which graphic novel would he get to enjoy first?

That's when I came into Michael's office, and asked him "Heads or tails?" Michael picked "heads," I flipped a coin and it came up heads. I took the DISNEY FAIRIES graphic novel, left him with the GERONIMO STILTON graphic novel, and told him as soon as he read the GERONIMO STILTON graphic novel, he could get the DISNEY FAIRIES graphic novel. Problem solved. That is until Papercutz publisher Terry Nantier came into Michael's office and announced that copies of the new NANCY DREW and HARDY BOYS graphic novels just came in from the printers!

"MOLDY MOZZARELLA!" Michael exclaimed, "Now what do I do?!"
I quickly asked Michael, "Heads or tails?"

One of the great things about graphic novels is that once you have them, you can enjoy them whenever you want, as many times as you want. And in any order you like.

To find out more about Papercutz graphic novels, visit www.papercutz.com.

For a sneak preview of GERONIMO STILTON Graphic Novel #6 "Who Stole the Mona Lisa?" just turn the page.

So, until next time, beware of any pussycats trying to sell you the world-famous Mona Lisa painting—chances are it might be hot!

Jim

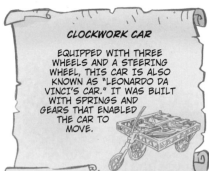

CLOCKWORK CAR

EQUIPPED WITH THREE WHEELS AND A STEERING WHEEL, THIS CAR IS ALSO KNOWN AS "LEONARDO DA VINCI'S CAR." IT WAS BUILT WITH SPRINGS AND GEARS THAT ENABLED THE CAR TO MOVE.

BATTISTA MENTIONED TO ME THAT YOU'RE ALSO **PAINTERS!**

ACTUALLY WE'RE JUST HUMBLE BEGINNERS!

WE WANT YOU TO TEACH US ALL YOUR PAINTING SECRETS!

I'M SORRY TO DISAPPOINT YOU, BUT I SELDOM DO ANY PAINTING NOW!

HOWEVER, I DO NEED ASSISTANTS TO TEST-DRIVE MY MACHINES!

UH-OH!

UM...>GLUB<...WE'D BE HONORED!

BUT I'M WARNING YOU: IT'S VERY DANGEROUS WORK!

WE CA...>AHEM< RODENTS ARE AFRAID OF NOTHING!

THEN YOU CAN HELP ME WITH MY EXPERIMENTS AND I'LL GIVE YOU PAINTING LESSONS IN EXCHANGE!

IT'S A DEAL!

HMM...I PREDICT A **SEA** OF TROUBLES!

IN THE MEANTIME, MY FRIENDS AND I HAD ALSO ARRIVED NEAR AMBOISE.

NICE LANDING, TRAP!

THANKS, COUSIN! YOU'RE TOO KIND!

ACTUALLY... I WAS BEING SARCASTIC!

WELL, WE'RE SAFE AND SOUND, RIGHT?

YES, BUT WE'RE AT THE TOP OF A TREE!

SO? THIS WAY WE WON'T EVEN HAVE TO HIDE THE SPEEDRAT!

BUT I'M AFRAID OF HEIGHTS! HOW AM I SUPPOSED TO GET DOWN?

YOU DON'T WANT ME TO CARRY YOU ON MY BACK, DO YOU, COUSIN?

WHILE YOU FINISH UP YOUR DISCUSSION, I'M *LEAVING*...

?!?

WOW! WHAT A RAT-TASTIC **LEAP!**

>GULP!<

AFTER WE ALL CLIMBED OUT AND WERE GETTING READY...

DON'T FORGET TO PUT ON PROFESSOR VOLT'S EARPHONES!

ARE WE GOING STRAIGHT TO THE CASTLE OF CLOUX, UNCLE GERONIMO?

YES, LEONARDO IS OUR ONLY **CLUE!**

LET'S GET GOING THEN!

HOW EXCITING: WE'RE IN THE HIGH RENAISSANCE!

AND SOON WE'LL EVEN MEET LEONARDO DA VINCI!

THIS IS THE CASTLE OF AMBOISE! CLOUX IS A LITTLE FARTHER ON!

AMBOISE CASTLE

WAS BUILT IN THE 13TH CENTURY ON A BLUFF OVERLOOKING THE LOIRE RIVER IN CENTRAL FRANCE. IN THE FOLLOWING CENTURIES, LARGE GARDENS AND WIDE BALCONIES WERE CREATED HANGING OVER THE RIVER. KING FRANCIS I OF FRANCE USED AMBOISE CASTLE AS HIS HOME WHEN HE STAYED IN THE LOIRE VALLEY.

A LITTLE LATER, WE REACHED THE CASTLE OF CLOUX.

STRANGE, NO ONE SEEMS TO BE **AROUND...**

I'LL TRY KNOCKING ON THE DOOR!

BUT... WE CAN'T DISTURB LEONARDO WITHOUT A REASON!

GERONIMO, YOU TOLD US LEONARDO WAS OUR ONLY CLUE!

Panel 1:
I KNOW, BUT... WHAT ARE WE GOING TO SAY TO LEONARDO?

I DON'T KNOW, BUT WE HAVE TO START LOOKING FOR THE CATS SOME- WHERE!

Panel 2:
AHOY THERE, WATCH OUT BELOW!

?!?

Panel 3 (SBAM):
SQUEAK!

WINGS

AMONG HIS VARIOUS DIFFERENT INVENTIONS, LEONARDO ALSO DESIGNED WINGS FOR FLYING THAT WERE LIKE THE WINGS OF A BAT AND COULD BE ATTACHED TO A FLYING MACHINE. ALL THE WINGS WERE MADE OF FABRIC STRETCHED OVER PANELS OF WOOD AND BAMBOO CANES.

CRISPY CRACKERS! GERONIMO STILTON!

POOR UNCLE! HE HIT HIM!

OWIEOWIE OWIEOWIE!

SOME- BODY'S BEEN HURT?

NO, NOT EVEN A SCRATCH!

OHH...!

EXCUSE ME... WOULD YOU MIND TELLING ME WHO YOU ARE?

MY NAME IS STIL... THAT IS, STILTONEAUX, GEROME STILTONEAUX!

Don't miss GERONIMO STILTON Graphic Novel #6 – "Who Stole the Mona Lisa?"

56

TH-TH-THERE IT IS...THAT'S IT!

UM...I GUESS WE'LL HAVE TO WAIT UP HERE!

GRRRR!

THE PIRATE CATS TRAVEL TO THE PAST ON THE CATJET SO THAT THEY CAN CHANGE HISTORY AND BECOME RICH AND FAMOUS. BUT GERONIMO AND THE STILTON FAMILY ALWAYS MANAGE TO UNMASK THEM!

CATJET

QUICK, LET'S CLIMB UP THIS TREE!